MY RED UMBRELLA

BY
ROBERT BRIGHT

for Susan

WILLIAM MORROW AND COMPANY, INC.
NEW YORK

Maybe I shouldn't have bothered
to bring my red umbrella.

But you never can tell.

Oh! Oh!

Here comes the rain.

And here's a little dog to walk with me
under my red umbrella.

And two kittens.

And three chickens.

And four little rabbits.

And a woolly lamb.

And two goats.

And three little pigs.

And four little foxes.

And a big wet bear.

All under my red umbrella.

So we all sing a rain song.
All around us everyone
is singing in the rain.

Until it begins to stop.

And the big bear goes home,
and the four little foxes.

And the three little pigs.

And the two goats
and the woolly lamb go home.

And the four little rabbits
and the three chickens.

And the two little kittens.

Everybody goes home.

And I go home
with my red umbrella.

Now I think it's a good thing
I brought it.